SUPER LEXI

Super LEXI

by Emma Lesko
Illustrated by
Adam Winsor

RED LEATHER BOOKS, LLC.

Blah blah blah

Text copyright © 2014 by Emma Lesko
Illustrations copyright © 2014 by Adam Winsor
Interior design by Typeflow

First paperback edition in this format 2014

ISBN 978-0-9914310-0-7 (paperback)

The illustrations were painted in Photoshop.

Red Leather Books, LLC.
2713 Salk Avenue, Suite 250
Carlsbad, CA 92008

Learn more about Super Lexi at
www.EmmaLesko.com

For my guys, J & D

Contents

1

The Staring Eyeballs

I don't like banging on noisy instruments, I don't like songs that get stuck in my head, and I don't like eyeballs staring at me. That's how come I don't like music class. The other kids at school like music a lot. That's no biggie, though. Everybody's different from everybody, and I'm different about music.

Too bad my music teacher, Mr. Duncan, always says, "All kids like music, Lexi!"

That's how come I have to go to music class.

So a few weeks ago, I made a wish to skip it. I crossed my toes and fingers. That can't make a wish come true, but since I crossed my eyes, too, it did. I got to go to a doctor's appointment instead. I've been going to those a lot lately. I don't get shots, though. Instead, I have to do babyish math problems and draw pictures. That time, I was supposed to make up a story about a rubber finger puppet.

I said it was dead.

The doctor's office is the pits, but I'd go there any day instead of school. Christopher would, too. He said I was a lucky duck. Only it wasn't luck. I'd been practicing crossing my eyes for weeks.

It was superpowers.

So that's how come I was excited at music class for the first time ever. Guess why? I made a wish for all of school to be cancelled.

I crossed my eyes the whole time Mr. Duncan made us bang on instruments. I only have Mr. Duncan once a week, and that's good. He acts fake-happy a lot. I'm not a fan of that. Mr. Duncan bounced his head and waved a magic wand at us. He's supposed to wave a plain stick, but he didn't because he said we were making magic. Only we weren't.

It was extra noisy because Mr. Duncan got the bright idea to let Phoebe ring a bell three inches from my eardrum. She's a princess girl who wears sparkly stuff on her face. She was a big fan of that bell.

I had to clang a triangle every time Mr. Duncan pointed his fake magic wand at me. I crossed my eyes the whole time.

After I counted twenty-seven clangs, Mr. Duncan said, "Class, I have a surprise."

The whole class stopped banging stuff. It didn't sound quiet, though, on account of everybody squealed and got wiggly. Except for me. I know teachers don't tell surprises to squealing kids. I sat very still like an ice cube.

Christopher squealed most of all. I'm his friend, but he's not my friend because sometimes he calls me "dumb-dumb." I tried to be stiff so he wouldn't notice me. His fingers got very inside my personal space anyway. "What do you think the surprise is, Lexi?" he asked. His breath smelled like milk.

I crossed my eyes at him.

I knew the surprise. School was going to get cancelled. That's how come I was thinking about the tornado twirls I was going to practice at home. I invented them. If you do them fast enough, you turn invisible. I was finally going to get enough time to practice. Then I'd have even more superpowers.

"One, two, three, eyes on me," said Mr. Duncan.

"One, two, eyes on you," we said, because those are the rules.

"We're going to have a celebration for Parents' Day. Who can guess what it is?"

My insides got quite squirmy. I don't like answering questions, but I do like being right. One of my doctors got curious about that once. I guess that's an interesting part of me.

When Mr. Duncan gets amazed, he says he's going to flip upside-down. Then he never actually does. That day, I was going to make him flip upside-down for real. I raised my hand because I don't blurt.

Kaylee yelled, "Eat brains!" She blabs about brains because zombies are her favorite. Even though blurters are not for me, I don't dislike Kaylee. She gets my crayons back from Christopher when he steals them. Plus, she only wears boys' clothes.

Actually, I am a fan of Kaylee.

Blurting's against the rules, but Mr. Duncan didn't move Kaylee's clip to the big, fat trouble clipboard like he's supposed to. He just said, "Kaylee, please raise your hand."

I stretched my arm as far up as I could. Then Christopher sat up on his knees. That's cheating because that's not bottoms-in-seats. His hand was higher than mine, so Mr. Duncan called on him.

"Are we going to eat brains?" Christopher asked.

"Copycat!" whispered Kaylee.

"No, Christopher, we're not eating brains. Lexi, you're raising your hand nicely. What do you think the celebration will be?"

Sometimes, my thoughts disappear when I get called on. I have phobias of lots of things, like yogurt, songs that get stuck in my head, and cashiers who think they're good with kids. My biggest phobia on all of Planet Earth, though, is eyeballs staring at me. When that happens, I feel like my scalp is shrinking and my hair is growing, all at the same time. Plus my brain freezes hard like an ice cube. Plus I get a feeling of barf. Plus, sometimes I do barf.

For a second, I forgot what I was going to say on account of everything inside my skull was frozen solid. Then I remembered. I got that happy feeling all over again. "You're going to cancel school," I said.

I waited for Mr. Duncan to flip upside-down.

Except he didn't.

He didn't even answer me.

He laughed.

After he laughed, all the kids did, too. It hurt my ears. My head felt like ants were crawling all over it. I crossed my eyes hard.

When Mr. Duncan finally talked, he said, "We're going to give a musical performance!"

Everyone cheered and clapped loudly. Except for me. I covered my ears. Then Mr. Duncan said the worst news ever. "We'll have to work very hard. So we'll have music class every day for two whole weeks!"

That place went bonkers. I was the only miserable person in the whole entire class. I got a feeling of "argh!" When I get that feeling, bad things happen. Like I forget I'm in school . . . and I crawl under my chair . . .

and I curl up like a roly-poly . . . and I cover my ears . . . in front of everybody.

So unfortunately, I did all that.

Also unfortunately, Phoebe rang her bell and yelled, "Mr. Duncan! Mr. Duncan! Look at Lexi!"

All of a sudden, I remembered I was doing all that stuff. Real quiet, I told my frozen brain, "You better get your bottom in your seat."

Except, breaking news.

It was too late.

Everybody's eyeballs were already staring at me.

2

The Barfy Pudding

After music class, lunchtime came. The kids in my class are supposed to sit at the same table, but I have special permission to sit by myself. Special permission is the only time I can break the rules without getting a feeling of barf. I got that permission because lots of lunches smell bad, so I need my distance. Lots of kids smell bad, too. Plus, they squish me and their elbows end up very inside my personal space. I am not a fan of that.

So even though I'm in second grade, I sit at the fourth grade lunch table without any fourth graders. They don't show up until it's time to throw my leftovers in the trash compactor, which I never do. That thing is another one of my phobias. I'm pretty sure it could smash a kid.

I was happy about lunch because a great idea popped into my skull. I was going to eat something slimy like snots to make me barf. After that, I'd get to go home sick and miss school. Then I'd get special permission to skip the music program. I couldn't wait to see if my mom packed something terrifying like yogurt or applesauce.

Only there was one problem. When I opened my lunch box, I didn't see any yucky food. All I had was an apple, a turkey sandwich, potato chips, and a bag of my daddy's homemade chocolate chip cookies. Those things are all either crunchy or tasty and not even a little bit like snots.

That's when I noticed Kaylee's pudding cup next to her crumply lunch bag. It was a weird yellow color, like foot blisters. I almost barfed looking at it. If I ate that stuff, I'd get to stay home for weeks.

I had to have it.

Lots of kids traded food at lunch, but I never did on account of no one ever asked me to. I knew I could get Kaylee to ask for my cookies, though. They looked so delicious that my mouth squirted drool inside because it wanted to eat them.

I stared at her pudding a real long time and waited for her to ask. Except she didn't even notice. She was sitting with our class, yelling at Christopher about the cheese puff crumbs that flew out of his mouth when he talked.

"How are you, Lexi?" I heard all of a sudden, and I jumped a little. I'm a very jumpy person. The talking person was this lady whose name I don't know. She always carries a big sponge and a bucket of cold, brown water. I stuck my finger in it once. Her job is to wipe down the tables with germs, I guess.

"How are you, Lexi?" she asked again.

The bad thing about cafeteria seats is that they are hard circles attached to the tables. They don't scoot. I was stuck.

She set her bucket in front of me. Dirty water slopped and spread germs in the air. "What do you say you try to sit with your grade today?" she asked.

"No thank you," I said.

"Just for a little."

Just then Kaylee threw her scrunched-up crusts at Christopher. He got revenge by squirting a juice box at her. The lady whose name I don't know didn't see it on account of she was staring at me.

"You're missing breaking news," I said.

"Where?"

I pointed at my class. I crossed my eyes and wished for the pudding.

"Guess I missed it," she said.

I uncrossed my eyes. That trick was hopeless.

"How about we try to get some kids to play four-square with you today?" she asked.

This conversation happened a lot. I was used to ignoring it. That time, I interrupted it because Kaylee grabbed her pudding and stood up. I snatched up my delicious cookies. All of a sudden, my mouth wanted to eat them again. I was sad it wouldn't get to. They were my only hope for barfing.

Before I could go up to Kaylee, Christopher chased her all the way to the trash compactor. "Walk!" said a lady who sells milk.

For a second, all I could think about was getting smooshed in the garbage squisher. I tried to get close to Kaylee without getting near that thing. I stopped by Milk Lady. I could smell the stink from there. I think of all the places to get smooshed, a pile of slobbery old kid food would be the worst.

I stretched out my leg to get closer, but not too close. Then I said, "Want my cookies?"

"What's wrong with them?" asked Kaylee.

"They're delicious," I said very quietly.

Kaylee did a shrug. "Sure."

I threw them at her. They bounced off her chest.

Milk Lady said, "No throwing food in the cafeteria."

I didn't answer. I'd probably never have to do that again, so what's the point.

Kaylee picked the cookies up off the floor and said, "Thanks, Lexi." Then she shoved them all into her mouth. I felt jealous about that. I would have done a better job of savoring them. That means I would have enjoyed them lots more.

I waited for her to toss her pudding at me.

Only she didn't.

Instead, she wound up her arm like a baseball pitcher and threw it into the trash compactor so hard that it banged in there.

3

My Slammed-Shut Mouth

The next day at school, nobody said anything about the music program, so I was pretty sure everyone forgot about it. I was very happy about that news and started to forget it myself. The morning was good on account of we had practice math tests, so nobody made a peep or else they'd get in big, fat trouble. Then I survived recess, which is breaking news.

The best part of the whole day, though,

was that it was Wednesday. After recess on Wednesdays comes the only part about school that I love love love.

Silent reading.

Silent reading is relaxing and it's fun and it's cozy, and I wish it could last forever. I'm actually very good at reading. I taught myself when I was three. My parents didn't even know until I surprised them.

I'm not supposed to tell anybody that story on account of it's not humble. Everybody learns to read in different ways. That's the way I learned, though. That's how come I'm a fan of silent reading.

My book still smelled new because I just got it from book orders. I picked it because the girl on the cover did not brush her hair. Also, she was not wearing pink. I was a fan of that girl.

I read my book while my regular teacher, Ms. Kleinert, talked at us. She's more peaceful than Mr. Duncan. She says the same thing in a quiet voice every Wednesday after recess: "Class, settle down and find your books." When I read it's easy for me not to hear words, so Ms. Kleinert's speech didn't interrupt me.

That's how come I was surprised when I felt her hand on my shoulder. "Lexi, did you hear me?"

"Yes," I said.

"What did I say?"

"I don't know," I said. "I heard your voice, not words."

The thing about Ms. Kleinert is she touches my chin so she can stare in my eyeballs when she talks. I'm actually not a fan of that. So, I looked at the hand that wasn't touching me. She had white chalk all over her finger and thumb.

"I said that silent reading is cancelled today," she said. "You're going to music class to practice the play."

That's when I had a crisis. A "crisis" is the grown-up word for the biggest problem on Planet Earth. I couldn't do anything about it, though. Ms. Kleinert was already on her way to lead the line. I had to line up, or else.

Practice wasn't in the music room. We passed right by it. We went single-file down a long hall, then zigzagged through a secret passageway. That got everybody squealy except for me. Then all of a sudden, we were on a stage, and we were staring at the empty cafeteria tables.

Some of the girls started dancing right away on account of I guess that's what stages are for. I was busy being confused because I never knew there was a stage in that place.

Nobody was in the whole cafeteria. It was dark out there. The trash compactor's scary mouth was closed shut. It looked like a frown.

Somehow Ms. Kleinert had disappeared, and my music teacher, Mr. Duncan, was handing me a stack of papers. "Please hand these out, Lexi," he said. I took my job very seriously, while he blabbed about scripts and new songs. Kids were already singing songs in their pages even though we didn't learn how yet. Plus, they were yelling stuff.

Braden said, "Kaylee, you're going to be the troll!"

Kaylee said, "Am not! I'm going to be a zombie that eats your brains!"

Phoebe said, "Is there a princess?"

Lots of other kids said stuff like that, too.

It sounded like a big party in there. I don't know what I'm supposed to do at parties so I sat on the floor. I'm lucky. I can do criss-cross applesauce anywhere because I don't wear skirts.

Mr. Duncan took one hundred hours to figure out who played what character. I got stuck with the troll on account of no one raised their hand for that one. Then Mr. Duncan arranged kids all over the stage. He made me stand on an X made out of purple tape.

The kids were super loud by then so I read my script on account of I was going to get my silent reading one way or another. It was a babyish story about goats. They were scared of a troll that lived under a bridge. I felt a little sad about being the bad guy.

That's when we had oral reading, which is not fun like silent reading. Oral reading is out loud with eyeballs staring at you. Everybody took turns except for me, on account of I didn't have a turn for a long time. The warm lights made my purple X feel like a sunny spot. For a while, I felt relaxed.

Then the whole place got silent.

"Lexi?" said Mr. Duncan.

I looked at him.

"Please read your lines."

My sunny spot felt too hot all of a sudden. I didn't know what page those people were on.

I got the feeling "argh!" Phoebe, the know-it-all, leaned over and flipped my pages for me. The bow on her headband tickled my face.

I looked at that crummy page and felt my eyebrows squeeze together. The whole page was filled with troll words, and I was supposed to say them out loud. My mouth didn't say words, though. It stayed shut in a frown like the trash compactor.

"Lexi, please read your lines," said Mr. Duncan.

My mouth did not open.

"She can't read," said Christopher.

"Everybody's good at different things, so stuff it," said Kaylee.

Mr. Duncan shushed them. "Lexi, you have a choice. Either you read your lines or stay inside for afternoon recess."

That was the most thoughtful thing anyone said to me all day. Recess was one of my phobias. I never played. At first my mouth wanted to stay shut, but then it let me whisper. "I choose door number two." "Door" can be a synonym for "choice."

Everybody's eyeballs stared at me on account of all kids are supposed to like recess, I guess.

"OK, Lexi, you'll have to read quietly in the office while your classmates play on the playground," said Mr. Duncan.

I felt very thankful about that favor.

4

The Top-Secret Plan

"Lexi, slow down. You'll get dizzy," said my mom.

I was practicing tornado twirls in the living room. That's a fancy room with hard couches that nobody sits on. It's the kind of room that stains when you bring juice in it, but who wants juice in there anyway because there's no TV. Besides, if you do it, you get in big, fat trouble. I don't know what big, fat trouble actually is because I don't break rules.

Pretty much all anyone's allowed to do in that living room is be bored.

Except when it's raining.

When it's raining, my mom moves the hard couches so there's a big open space. Then she says, "Get those wiggles out, you're driving me nuts!"

I'm an inside kid. Tornado twirls only fit inside on rainy days, so I felt happy. It would have been perfect, except for one problem. The thing with tornado twirls is you need your concentration. That means no moms talking at you.

"I mean it, Lexi. Take your time."

"I'm getting invisible," I said and went faster.

My mom blew her breath loudly. I

wondered how much carbon dioxide was near me now. Carbon dioxide is the air people breathe out and plants breathe in. I read about it in my almanac. "Your carbon dioxide is breaking my concentration," I said.

Even though I was tornado twirling at

blur speed, I knew she was digging in my backpack. I heard it unzip. So, I went faster. I wanted to disappear before she found the blue paper I had to put in there. I knew I was too late when she said, "A Parents' Night program! You're going to be a troll!"

"That's fiction," I said, which is the grown-up word for "lie."

"Why?"

"Can you see me?" I asked.

"Yes, I can see you, Lexi. Why is this fiction?" She pointed at the blue paper.

"Darn." I tornado twirled faster.

She breathed slowly like I'm supposed to when I need to calm down. Then she caught me in the middle of a tornado twirl, and plopped me on the couch. The cushion was even harder than I remembered. The room was spinning and was quite blurry.

"How did you do that?" I asked.

"Lexi, look at me."

All of a sudden, my eyeballs wanted to look at my pants. I got a hole in the knee because someone knocked me over at dismissal.

My pants' hole was actually a big scrape made out of little holes. They were shaped like parallelograms. Those are like rectangles, only they're squashed and slanted. Parallelograms are practically a college shape, and I know all about them.

"Lexi, why aren't you going to be a troll?"

"I choose silent reading."

"That's not a choice, Lexi."

This was breaking news.

"Don't you like trolls?" she asked.

I counted my parallelograms even though they were still spinning a little, too. There were sixteen.

"I thought you'd be excited. You love lep-rechauns," she said.

"They aren't the same thing," I said. If they were, I'd be the happiest kid on Plan-et Earth because leprechauns can do magic. Plus, they have lots of money. Also, they can turn themselves invisible. I would very much like to be one.

"You're right," she said. "They're not the same. They're similar."

This was also breaking news. "Can trolls make themselves invisible?" I asked.

"Maybe. You have poetic license."

"I do not know those words."

She explained about poetic license. It means I could make my troll however I wanted. I didn't listen, though. The rain got loud so my ears were busy. I started think-ing about how the sun would come out later and how it would smell like wet cement and worms. There would be a rainbow. Then the leprechauns would come out to play.

That's when a secret popped into my brain.

"I need to make something now," I said.

"Lexi, I was talking. Did you hear what I said?"

"Can I use glitter?" Glitter is an outside toy because it's a big fat mess. I needed special permission to use it inside.

"Your teacher wants you to practice your lines and review math facts. Which would you like to do first?"

"Nor."

"Neither is not one of your choices."

I rubbed the parallelograms with my finger. They felt quite bumpy.

"Lexi? What do you choose?"

"Glitter."

She did a taking-a-break breath again. It smelled like carbon dioxide and white gum. "If you do your homework, you can use it, but it does not leave the kitchen. Got it?"

All of a sudden, I got happy. I had a plan.

5

Sparkly Things and Junky Cereal

First, I found shiny things—all kinds of shiny things, like quarters and nickels and sparkly rocks from my collection. Then I got an inspiration, which is a great idea. I dumped all of my rocks out of my secret, private shoebox. I took the box to the kitchen table because of the glitter rule. That was too bad, because I needed privacy. Mom was in there. The only good thing was that she was cooking a dinner that smelled like spaghetti, which is much better than smelling like dry, chewy steak.

I turned on all the lights, even the buzzy ones that make my head dizzy. I wanted to see very well. I squirted glue all over the box, stuck cotton balls on it, and sprinkled gold glitter everywhere. It looked like a sparkly cloud.

Then came the most important part.

"What's the rainbow colors?" I asked.

"ROYGBIV. You sure are busy over there," said Mom.

ROYGBIV is what my mom says when I'm supposed to figure out the rainbow colors myself. I know the answer. I learned it in pre-school: red, orange, yellow, green, blue, indigo, violet. It's just easier if my mom says it.

"I don't have an indigo crayon," I said.

"Use dark blue."

"Dark blue is not indigo," I said.

"What are you working on?"

"Nothing." "Nothing" does not actually mean "nothing" all the time. Sometimes it means "something very special and private."

"What colors make indigo?" I asked.

"Purple and blue."

Just then Daddy walked in and let blustery air blow in. My cotton balls fluttered but didn't blow off because I glued them very strong. My daddy had a drippy umbrella in his hand. It got my leg wet when he kissed me "hello." I wiped his wet off me with my sleeve.

"Lexi, can you say 'hi' to your dad?" asked my mom. I didn't hear her too well because I was making indigo.

"That's quite a diorama," said Daddy.

"I don't know what that is."

"A little scene," he said.

"I need cereal with marshmallows in it," I said.

"Junky cereal's for birthdays," said Daddy.

"I need it for my project."

"What is this project?" He looked at it quite closely. I covered it with my arms and hair. Even though I'm officially a tomboy, I have long, girly hair because scissors are not for me. Mostly, it's knots because brushes are not for me either. It covers up secret projects very well.

My mom kissed Daddy "hello." Then she said, "If I have to go to the store to buy junky cereal, I want to know what it's for."

I breathed loudly and put my head on the table. I do that when I don't want to talk. For a while, the only noise was from Mom banging the pans and Daddy blabbing about his day. When Mom poured the noodle water into the sink, I figured out the subject had been dropped.

I breathed out as loudly as I could.

"Stop kicking the chair, please," said Mom.

"Well, I didn't know I was doing that," I said.

"And wash your hands for dinner."

"It was supposed to be private, but apparently I don't have a choice," I said. I huffed because I wanted my parents to know I had strong anger. That's one of the feelings on my feelings poster. I'm supposed to point to it instead of huffing. "It's a leprechaun trap," I said.

Leprechauns are little like your thumb, and they're troublemakers. They're very cute pets. If you catch one, you get to choose between lots of money or magic powers. I was going to choose magic powers so I could disappear during the school program. The problem was, after we got my guinea pig, Fred, the rules were no more pets. I crossed my eyes and wished for my parents to forget that rule.

"Aren't leprechauns supposed to be impossible to catch?" asked Daddy.

"You don't understand," I said.

"Help me understand," he said. I couldn't, though. If he knew I was going to escape the Parents' Day program, he would keep it from happening.

My body threw itself off the chair and lay on the floor. It felt very angry about all this pressure. The floor didn't help. The tiles were cold, and I am a very chilly person. I scooted to the rug like an inchworm and put my face on it. The rug is not as soft on faces as it looks.

"I curse you!" I said.

"Lexi, what did we tell you about cursing people?" asked Mom.

I did not curse people. I cursed the rug.

The next thing I knew, my mom was on her knees and very inside my personal space. She took off her oven mitt and put her hand on my cheek. "What's the cereal for?" she asked peacefully.

I growled and put my hands over my eyes.

Tears tried to squeeze out. She stared at me. That made me feel like barf.

My hands got very tight in fists. "Bait!" I finally said.

"Maybe we could use some candy from home for bait," said my mom.

"It has to have rainbow marshmallows in it!" I said. My voice squeaked because now the tears were out. They made my throat weird. I wanted to tell her I saw it in a commercial, but everything was stuck.

She patted my back and said, "OK. That makes sense. Now was that so hard?"

"Yes." I wiped my face with the rug, and it scratched me.

She stood up and walked away. Daddy clanged silverware. Mom rinsed the noodles. No one said they'd buy marshmallow cereal.

Still lying on the floor and still very angry,

I kicked my shoes off. I crossed my toes. I crossed my fingers. I crossed my hairs.

Then I crossed my eyeballs.

My dad's feet stepped over me while he set the table. My guinea pig Fred nibbled on alfalfa hay. My mom slopped spaghetti onto our plates. My insides felt furious and hard like an ice cube.

"Can't I pay for it with my own money?" I asked, quite growly.

My mom blew carbon dioxide all over the place. "I'll pick some up tomorrow," she said.

That's how my superpowers started working again.

6

The Most Famous Kid
on Planet Earth

Normally at creative writing time at school, I leave my page blank. That's because my imagination is blank. Ms. Kleinert says everybody has an imagination. Even one of my doctors blabbed about imaginations. I told him what I tell all grown-ups who blab about them: I don't have one.

After my superpowers started working again things were different. A nonfiction story popped in my head. It didn't take any imagination, though, because "nonfiction" means "true." I also had an idea for a picture, which Ms. Kleinert calls an illustration. I got to work right away.

The other kids get excited during creative writing. It's a noisy time, even though we're supposed to be silent until 10:15, when all the kids except me raise their hands to read their stories. Kaylee never follows that rule. I'm in desk fourteen, and she sits at desk fifteen. She always tells me her story before it's time. Her story was about Ms. Kleinert breaking into her house and stealing cookie dough. I don't know if it was fiction or not. It made me laugh inside. I did not laugh on the outside, because Ms. Kleinert was trying to find the quietest student.

Ms. Kleinert doesn't help us spell because

she wants us to sound it out. She just walks around and tells us "good job." When she got to the back row, she told the class that she liked how quietly I was working.

Everybody turned their eyeballs at me, which I normally don't like, but that time I felt warm inside. I looked at the chew marks on my pencil.

"What's your picture?" asked Kaylee.

I raised my hand and accidentally hit Ms. Kleinert's pants.

"Yes, Lexi?"

"How do you spell 'leprechaun trap'?" I asked.

"How do you think you spell it?" she asked, which is not a good question. If I knew that answer, I wouldn't ask.

Ms. Kleinert told the whole class we were getting marbles in our jar because we were such hard workers. A jar full of marbles equals Gum Chewing Day. I thought everybody should be grateful to me for that favor because I was the quietest. After that, the whole class shushed like they always do when marbles get in the jar. My head felt quite peaceful.

Since Ms. Kleinert doesn't give special permission for glitter, I used the gold crayon. It was still pointy.

Gold crayons have real gold flecks in them. If you press very hard, they color sparkly, so that's what I did. Normally I'm not a good drawer because my hands don't have much energy. That day, though, my picture was the kind that Ms. Kleinert writes on with words like "fabulous" or "wow." Pretty soon, my leprechaun trap picture sparkled almost as much as the real thing.

"Why does your mouth move when you color?" asked Kaylee.

I didn't actually know I was doing that. She was peeking, but I didn't hide my picture, because I felt proud.

"It's really pretty, Lexi! What is it?" she asked.

I had a dilemma. A "dilemma" is a grown-up word for having no idea what you're supposed to do. The rules are no whispering, but the words were tickling my insides. They wanted out. I frowned to keep them in me, but they escaped. "I'm getting a leprechaun," I whispered. "His name is Leppy, and he's going to teach me magic."

"Lucky!" she said.

Ms. Kleinert said "Shush!" to her.

So we shushed, but the words were still in my head. They were happy words, and they moved at blur speed. My insides felt like I drank hot chocolate.

I got that feeling once when my mom made me bring my guinea pig Fred for pre-school show-and-tell. I was famous. All the kids wanted to come over for play dates, which was good because "play dates" is always on my sticker chart. That's where my mom writes a list of stuff I don't want to do, then she gives me prizes when I do them. I never actually agreed to that. I was about to get a whole lot of sticker chart prizes soon, though.

After I told my class about Leppy, I was going to be the most famous kid on Planet Earth.

7

"Nonfiction" Means "True"

It seemed like a hundred hours before the little hand was on the ten and the big hand was on the three. That's how time works. It goes fast when you're doing tornado twirls, and it goes slowly when you wish it would hurry up. By the time we were allowed to read our stories, I had fizzy feelings all over my body.

Normally, I do math problems in my head

while Ms. Kleinert calls on volunteers, but that day was different. That day, I was a volunteer. I raised my hand. It took a long time for my turn to come. First we had to listen about Ruhan going to the Upper Peninsula. Then Avery told us about a babyish roller coaster at Cedar Point that she thought was for big kids. Then Jayden blabbed about his boring grandma.

Then finally, my turn came.

I had to go up to the front of the room. Everybody's eyeballs stared at me. No one wiggled. The only sound was from Isa's sniffle nose. My paper got fluttery, and my hands couldn't hold it still.

" 'My Leprechaun Trap,' by Lexi Gates," I said. My voice sounded weird.

"Today I will catch a leprechaun. He will be my pet. He will give me superpowers," I

read. I turned my paper to the class. I pointed at my picture and said, "This is the trap
I made. Leprechauns like sparkles and rainbows and cereal with marshmallows."

All the kids stared at me. My chest
thumped a lot. The lights buzzed. I looked

at my empty chair and wished I could sit in it. I couldn't, though. The rules are that you have to stand there until Ms. Kleinert says.

Finally, Kaylee said, "Can I come over and play with him?"

After that, all the kids stopped keeping their thoughts in their heads. I didn't know who said what. I heard things like "I love that cereal!" "I want a leprechaun!" "Can you really turn invisible?" I was famous.

Even Ms. Kleinert was proud of me.

"That's quite an imagination you have, Lexi."

"It's not imagination. It's nonfiction," I said.

"What's that?" asked Kaylee.

" 'Nonfiction' means 'true,' " said Ms. Kleinert.

"Dumb-dumb! Leprechauns don't get

caught!" said Christopher, the blurtface.

Normally, when a kid's clip gets moved, the whole class gets quiet. But that time, Christopher's clip got moved and the class got loud. Ms. Kleinert said, "One, two, three, eyes on me." Nobody except me said, "One, two, eyes on you." All the kids were blurting about their furniture getting moved around on St. Patrick's Day and their milk turning green. One kid even had green water in his toilet. But no one ever saw the leprechauns that did those things.

I stood as still as an ice cube and crossed my eyeballs. I wished I could disappear. Christopher blurted, "What's wrong with your eyes?"

The kids got louder. The room looked like it does when I do tornado twirls. Plus, every- thing looked double because my eyes were crossed. Time didn't work again. It felt like forever, and my eyeballs hurt. Finally, Ms. Kleinert rang her little bell, which meant all the kids were being bad. If you blurt after the bell, you get your clip moved, so no one did. That was a big relief.

"Lexi, that's quite a trick you're doing with your eyes. It looks to me like you already have some leprechaun powers," Ms. Kleinert said.

All of a sudden, I felt like I drank hot chocolate again.

8

The Recess Secret

Normally, recess is the time of day when I walk around, or lay in my sunny spot, or close my eyes and count to 2,400, because that's how many seconds until it ends. It's actually a terrible time of day. Except that day. That day, I didn't even think about doing those things. I was busy being famous with Kaylee.

It was a warm day. Some old leaves were

laying around. Kaylee and I made a tiny leaf pile with our hands by the fences, away from the kids. Jumping in leaves is not for me because they get stuck inside my clothes. Kaylee doesn't get scratchy, though. She didn't even feel the leaves that were stuck to her hair.

She does feel twigs, though, so she gave me the very important job of taking them out of the pile. There were eighteen so far. I organized them in six piles of three.

Kaylee was on worm patrol because the leaves were wet. "What kind of magic are you going to learn?" she asked.

"It's a secret," I said.

"But we're friends," said Kaylee. "Friends tell each other secrets."

"Actually, that is true," I said. I frowned so I wouldn't show my smile. Kaylee was my very first friend since I got Ms. Kleinert, and this was our very first time playing together. That was great news. "You have to promise not to tell," I said.

"Stick a needle in my eye," she said.

"I don't know why you said that."

"It means if I tell anyone, I have to stick a needle in my eye," she said.

"Actually, that's gross," I said. I straightened my stick piles before I stood up. Then I got close to Kaylee's ear even though no one was around. That's how you have to tell secrets. I whispered, "I'm going to turn invisible during the Parents' Day performance."

That got Kaylee excited. She covered her mouth and tried not to squeal, but squeals came out anyway. "I have to see that! When can I see you do that? Can I come over tomorrow?"

That would make my mom very happy.

"Yes," I said. "Leppy's teaching me. I'm getting him tonight."

After that, I had trouble keeping my happiness inside because Kaylee was celebrating. She threw leaves in the air and called them "confetti." The sun was warm, and the air smelled green like it does in spring. For a second, it was the best recess ever. I did seven tornado twirls in a row to show Kaylee I could already kind of make myself invisible. They were the fastest tornado twirls I'd ever done. "I'm a blur!" I said.

She said, "And soon, you'll disappear on stage!"

Then I said, "I'll be invisible!"

Then she said, "You'll have superpowers!"

Then a different voice said, "Dumb-dumb! Kids don't have superpowers! You can't make yourself invisible!"

That's how we found out Christopher was spying on us in the bushes. That's also how I found out my fastest tornado twirls don't make blurs. My insides got stiff like an ice cube. All of a sudden I got the feeling of barf.

"You shut up, you big dope, or I'll eat your brains!" said Kaylee.

"You're dumb-dumbs!" said Christopher. "You're not going to catch any leprechaun!"

"Is too!" said Kaylee. "Her mom said she could, so you shut up!"

I crossed my eyes and made a wish, but it didn't come true. Instead, Christopher hit the back of my head and said, "Now your eyes are stuck like that forever."

I stopped to see if he was right.

Luckily, he was not.

He kicked Kaylee's leaf pile and messed up my twigs. Inside, I told him to quit blowing his stinky carbon dioxide all over us. On the outside, my mouth was quiet and would not say anything.

Kaylee picked up one of her worms and chased him with it. Normally boys aren't scared of worms. Christopher was a scaredy-cat, though, because Kaylee yelled, "I'm going to put him in your ear, and he'll eat your brains!"

He ran to the blacktop. For a second, I thought Kaylee defeated him. Except then he yelled to all the kids, "Lexi thinks kids have superpowers. She thinks she's going to turn invisible on stage!"

That's how come I started to worry the Leppy plan might not work.

9

Lucky Thing Number Three

Rehearsal was worse that day on account of door number two was not one of my choices. I only had one choice, and that was to read and even sing with eyeballs staring at me. It was torture.

After school was the kind of afternoon when all you want to do is eat marshmallow cereal and play with your guinea pig

Fred. Instead, I had to go to another crummy doctor's appointment.

Usually my mom takes me, but this time my daddy went, too. We went to the same doctor who made me tell a story about a dead finger puppet. He said he didn't need to see me this time, which was the only lucky thing that happened since Christopher ruined the only recess I ever liked. My parents had to go in a room with him. I had to stay with a nurse lady.

"Have fun with your dead finger puppets," I said.

I ended up in the waiting room. The nurse lady gave me a box of apple juice. She didn't make me talk at all. Actually, I was a fan of that nurse lady. She let me watch a violent cartoon, which was lucky thing number two, and then we left.

At home that night, lucky thing number three didn't happen right away. I tried to eat Leppy's cereal, but that was against the rules on account of junk food is not for dinner. So, I had to eat dry, chewy steak instead.

I was scooting it away from my macaroni when my mom and daddy looked at me quite serious. Daddy said, "Lexi, we have to talk to you about something important."

I soaked up steak juice with my napkin so my plate was more sanitary, which is the grown-up word for "not gross."

"We found out why music class is so hard on you," said Mom.

"Because it's torture," I said.

"The thing is, Lexi, all people are different," she said.

"I've been telling you that for years." I borrowed my mom's napkin for more soaking.

"Sometimes grown-ups take a while to catch on."

"Can I have cereal?" I asked.

"Yes, healthy cereal. Lexi, can you look at me?" asked Mom.

I needed my eyes to look for cereal in the cupboard. My daddy started talking about the important thing.

"Lexi, all people's brains are unique."

I was very happy to discover that we had O's.

Daddy kept talking. "Your brain is the reason you are so smart and so honest. But for everything that comes easily to a person, there are also challenges. Do you know what a challenge is, Lexi?"

"Hard thing."

"Right. Because you have strengths, you also have challenges. For instance, it's hard for you to talk about your feelings or to look into people's eyes. One other challenge is that music is very loud for you."

"Duh," I said. I ripped the O's box and stuck a piece of the cardboard in Fred's cage.

"Lexi, because of the way your brain works, your ears hear sound louder than most people," said Mom.

"One, two, eyes on you," I said, because

that got my attention. "Do I have supersonic ears?"

"I guess so," she said.

My insides got quite happy, on account of everybody knows supersonic ears are a superpower. So Christopher was wrong. Kids could have superpowers! Maybe Leppy could teach me to turn invisible after all. Hooray for my brain.

10

Catching Leppy

When I woke up the next morning, the sun was still on the other side of Planet Earth. I had trouble sleeping on account of I didn't want to leave Leppy downstairs in his trap. I had a very nice cage waiting for him next to my bed. It's the one my guinea pig Fred lived in before he got big. I put sparkly things in it, plus a paper cup of marshmallow cereal, and a picture of a rainbow. Also, I made a bed out of soft cotton from the inside of my ripped zebra. That way, Leppy would feel at home.

I tiptoed downstairs. I wanted to play with him before anybody woke up. "I think the sound of his trap woke me up," I whispered quietly to myself. I listened for leprechaun noises. I only heard Fred chewing on his toilet paper roll.

The kitchen was pitch dark, and the tile froze my bare feet. "I am a very chilly person," I said to myself. I hugged my arms. Then all of a sudden I got that happy feeling. Guess why? The shoebox on Leppy's trap was not up like I left it. It was down!

I ran over to it because there was a leprechaun in there. I lifted the box very slowly. I stuck my fingers under it so Leppy could smell them. I learned to do that with Fred when he was new. Only I didn't feel Leppy's little nose.

"Come here, boy," I whispered sweetly. "You're OK." I lifted the box a little more and stuck my eye under it so I could see. The only light came from the moon. It wasn't enough. Finally, my hands got so sick of waiting that they flipped that box right over. Then I got a terrible feeling inside my skull.

Leppy was gone.

Later at school, Kaylee took the news quite well. "We can still have a play date," she said.

"I can't. I have to work hard on a new trap," I said. I wasn't looking at her. I was rubbing a quarter between my fingers because that's all little Leppy left behind before he ran away. It sparkled in the sun more than a normal quarter because leprechaun quarters are magic.

"I'll help!" said Kaylee.

"Do you have sparkly things?" I asked.

"My sister has lots of jewelry."

"That could work." I was speaking quietly, even though we were standing in line outside. I could scream and yell if I felt like it. It's just that screams and yells were not in me. Only quiet words were.

"Did he eat the cereal?" she asked.

"He made a mess of it. He threw it all over the table," I said.

"Maybe the marshmallows were too hard. I should bring squishy ones."

"Probably," I said. I picked at some gunk on Leppy's quarter.

"Does this mean you have to go to rehearsal today?" she asked.

My eyes burned a little about that. Trying to keep them dry made my throat achy. I nodded.

"What part's the worst, Lexi? Singing, dancing, or grown-ups staring at you?" Kaylee asked.

I could feel my face screw up because the cries were really in me. I knew crummy Christopher would call me a crybaby if he saw. Then everybody would look at me. The bell rang, and the kids started to line up.

Some of them bumped me. It took me a long time to answer that difficult question. When I finally did, my voice was a teensy squeak. "It's all terrible," I said.

"Idea alert." Kaylee put her hands on my shoulders. "Look in my eyes," she said.

I didn't because I was looking at her orange shoelaces.

"When everyone sings, move your mouth up and down and don't say any words. When there's dancing, go behind someone who is dancing and sneak behind the curtains. Then plug your ears."

"That's against the rules," I said.

"Not really," she said. "It's like resting up so you can do your solo!"

My eyes got wetter than ever. "It won't work," I said.

"Why not?" she asked.

I covered my face with my hands and Leppy's quarter, because that's the only thing left to do at a time like that. My voice was even teensier and squeakier than before. "My brain doesn't remember words when eyeballs stare at me!"

11

The Performance

Every night for two weeks I caught Leppy, and every night he ran away. At first he left quarters. Then nickels and pennies. On the day of the Parents' Day performance, he left a lucky silver dollar and a note:

This dollar's full of lots of luck
Though it's only worth a buck
Bring it up on stage today
Your worries will just melt away!

That's how come I had that dollar in the pocket of my raggedy troll pants up on stage when the performance began. I moved my mouth up and down to make it look like I was singing. Since it was the real performance and not a rehearsal, bright lights got in my eyes and hurt them. They were too hot, not warm like a sunny spot. I was sweating inside my itchy shirt even though I'm normally a very chilly person.

Plus, the blaring music hurt my ears.

The worst part was that somewhere behind all those lights, a million grown-up eyeballs stared at me. Even my parents' eyeballs. That made it hard for me to remember my troll dance. So I danced it wrong. Nick danced right onto my bare, troll foot.

"Scoot, Lexi!" he said. He danced around me.

I decided it was a good time to hide behind the curtain and cover my ears like Kaylee said. I crawled there.

The curtain felt soft and velvety on the front side, but not on the backside. That part itched like my troll shirt. Everything behind the curtain was different than the stage. Instead of bright lights, it was pitch dark, like inside my bedroom closet. Plus, there were no kids dancing and no cardboard trees. Just lots of junk like desks and chairs and a broom. I sat still like an ice cube because I didn't want to knock stuff over.

Even though I squished my hands hard against my ears, I could hear the singing. I decided that was the perfect time to have a conversation with my coin.

Magic coins understand English. If you ask right, they make wishes come true. So I took

Leppy's coin out of my troll pants and I held it real close to my mouth. "Please make me invisible, please make me invisible, please make me invisible," I said softly.

Christopher was a billy goat. The kids sang that he was walking toward the bridge. That meant very soon I'd have to dance around that bridge and sing, "I'm going to gobble you up."

I took a deep breath like I'm supposed to when I'm not calm. Then I crawled out of the curtains onto that bright, loud stage.

I had to blink extra times because the lightbulbs hurt me. My stomach had the feeling of barf. Then I noticed my arm in my troll shirt, which was the color of boogers. My forehead got the bad tingles.

I was not invisible.

I got desperate. Desperate is when you

want a wish so bad that you'll do anything.

Except I was out of things to do.

No one sang. Instead, they looked at me and waited because my turn was now.

Christopher whispered, "Talk, dummy." I knew I was supposed to say something, but I couldn't remember what that something was. All I could think about was how hot those bright lights were and how much my stomach felt like barf. Also, I was thinking about the eyeballs looking at me.

Kaylee whispered, "Say, 'I'm going to gobble you up.'"

I didn't say it, though. I couldn't. All of a sudden, I felt like a volcano. I was mad at my grown-ups for not listening to me. For making me get up on that stage, even though that stage was not for me. All kids do not like music. Everybody's different from

everybody, and I was different about that.

I did not belong there.

That's how come I decided to break the rules. I knew I'd get my clip moved. I knew I'd finally figure out what big, fat trouble meant. My stomach hurt a little bit about that, but thinking about my solo made it hurt more.

So I stood up. I held my Leppy coin tight. I took a deep breath like I'm supposed to do when I'm not calm.

Then I did a tornado twirl.

I did another.

Then another.

I tornado twirled at blur speed all the way across the stage, only I knew I wasn't a blur, and I didn't even care.

When I got to the edge, my whole head felt like I drank a milk shake too fast. My troll outfit felt sweaty. Christopher laughed. Everybody else froze like ice cubes, even the grown-ups. I looked at all of them and said very quietly, "That bridge is not for me." Then I tornado twirled again and again and again down the ramp and into the hall outside the cafeteria.

It was silent and peaceful in there.

All those tornado twirls made my arms and legs floppy. I plopped onto the cold floor and leaned on the brick wall. My head was dizzy. Plus, I still had the feeling of barf from breaking the rules. After I sat there for a few seconds, though, I noticed I had a new feeling. I made my wish come true all by myself, without superpowers and without good luck. I felt brave.

So, right before Mr. Duncan and my parents barged through the door, I got to enjoy my new feeling for a minute.

Then I barfed.

12

Hooray for Superpowers!

The thing about big, fat trouble is that you have to be prepared for it, which I wasn't, on account of the barfs. I got to go to the nurse's office. That's a secret room I never went to before. It had a little bed and even a bathroom with a kid-sized toilet that I wouldn't be afraid of drowning in. I thought the whole place was very cozy. I got to lay in the bed and sip on a ginger ale, which is a fizzy drink that tastes like when your foot falls asleep. Only it's delicious.

We stayed in there for a whole half a can of ginger ale. When my mom announced it didn't come back up, that meant the barfs were done and big, fat trouble was finally coming. Only nobody yelled. Instead, my daddy carried me out to the car like a baby, which I am not. I didn't mind, though. His shoulder can be the correct place for my face sometimes.

Daddy rolled the windows down so I could smell fresh air instead of car smell. Also, he turned off the AM radio so it wouldn't make me carsick. I thought that was unexpected treatment.

Everyone was very quiet because such a bad thing happened. Only it never would have happened if my grown-ups had just listened to me in the first place. That's how come I finally said, "Well. You really botched that."

My parents laughed as loud as an explosion.

"Except it's not funny," I said, on account of it traumatized me. "Traumatized me" means that I'll have this crummy memory until I'm as old as my grandparents.

Normally when my parents laugh at not-funny things, my insides get hard like an ice cube. That time, my insides waited to see why they were doing that.

"Life is an experiment," my mom finally said.

"I do not know those words," I said.

"It means in life we have to make decisions without always knowing the right answer. We guessed wrong about music, and we're sorry."

"One, two, eyes on you," I said. "Does that mean no more music class?"

"For now, yes," said my mom.

That's how I figured out the big, fat trouble was not coming after all. Even better, I figured out that sorry parents let their kids eat leprechaun cereal for dinner. Also, sorry parents pour themselves bowls of junky cereal even though they're health nuts. Sometimes you just need to celebrate the end of a bad thing.

My daddy put my cereal in the giant bowl I painted for him one Christmas. I was very happy to discover that I had five marshmallow rainbows right on top. My milk turned purple very quickly.

"It's a shame Leppy's not here to enjoy this," I said.

"It is," said my daddy. Only we didn't get

to miss him for long, because Fred squeaked in his cage and stood up on his back legs. That's when I realized that Fred never ran away once, and Leppy ran away fourteen times. I thought I wanted Leppy, but actually, I am a fan of Fred.

"Can Fred run around in his ball?" I asked. So, Daddy plopped him in there, while Mom and I slurped our milk.

Fred's indigo ball rolled around and bumped into our feet and the table legs. I teased him with my bare, troll toes.

All of sudden, it felt like a party in that kitchen. Normally I don't like parties because they are noisy, but I liked that one. I wanted it bigger.

"Can Kaylee come over and play with Fred?" I asked. "She likes little pets."

"Of course! I'll call her mother after

dinner," said my mom.

I got another bowl and poured Leppy's cereal for Kaylee, then I dug for extra rainbows for her. My brain started thinking about everything that happened over the last two weeks. I thought about how we found out I have supersonic ears, how I got my first Ms.-Kleinert's-class-friend, and I don't have to go to music class anymore. That made me want to share the secret that I was hiding inside my head.

"I have breaking news," I said.

My parents stopped eating and didn't move like the kids do when Ms. Kleinert yells, "Freeze!"

"I disappeared from stage!" I said. "And I didn't even need Leppy!"

My crazy daddy made a very shocked face and dropped his spoon onto the table,

even though he had milk in that spoon. That made my insides quite happy.

"Do you think Leppy gave me powers after all?" I asked.

"I think it's because you are the most determined kid I know," said Daddy. "And that's a superpower."

I felt like throwing old leaves in the air like confetti, but they were outside and I wasn't. So instead, I stood up on my chair and wiggled my bottom. "I have superpowers!" I sang. I did a little troll dance up there on that chair, and I didn't even dislike that dance.

My mom and daddy didn't say that chairs are for sitting on. Instead, my crazy daddy got up on his chair and wiggled his bottom, too. Then he tugged my mom's elbow. She said she didn't want to, but that was fiction, because she got up on her chair and wiggled her bottom, too.

Then we all sang, "Hooray for superpowers!"

Check out

www.EmmaLesko.com

for Lexi's:

- Word Games
- Gross-Out Pranks
- Video Games
- Contests
- Kid Recipes
- Free Stuff

Don't miss Lexi's next book:

SUPER LEXI

is not a fan of Christmas

Coming in the fall, 2014!

Emma Lesko

grew up near Detroit, Michigan, where she ate dirt, taught her guinea pig to turn the basement lights on with his teeth, and read books in a garbage can. Like all kids, Emma had some superpowers. She had supersonic ears, super-strong taste buds and a super-smelling nose. Sometimes her superpowers were spectacular, and sometimes they gave her a feeling of barf. Though Emma has written a gazillion kids' stories, this is the first one she ever showed anybody.

Adam Winsor

grew up near Raleigh, North Carolina, where he explored the forest, drew comic books, and collected dead bugs from those filter holes in the sides of the swimming pool. He despised music class, hated eyeballs staring at him, and in the middle of one performance, wrapped himself entirely in the American flag he was holding so that no one would see his face. He has worked on several illustration and animation projects for kids, but this is the first chapter book.

CPSIA information can be obtained at www.ICGtesting.com
Printed in the USA
LVOW06s2326060814

397942LV00004B/232/P